THIS BOOK BELONGS TO:

Enjoy!

April 2011

WHAT OTHERS ARE SAYING ...

The **artist Nilda Comas** *about The Tale of the Little Duckling,*

"This book will delight children for its simple narrative and bright illustrations. Children will fall in love with the character and will love the adventures. It has sweetness in its delivery as if it were written with the spontaneity of a child. The approach will not intimidate a child and will encourage the child to have the whole book read to him. It is the kind of book that a child could want to retell himself after having heard it because the illustrations will inspire them to make their own stories."

The **teacher Irene Szymanski** *about Lollopy-and-Friends books,*

"These are great and lovely stories with fine eye-catching illustrations. The books are worth reading not only for children but for adults, too. Friendship, hope and how to overcome problems together are main themes of the books. They educate children and make them familiar to different topics of our everyday lives. We all, especially children, want to find out who we are. While looking at the pictures, reading the stories and reflecting them we have fun, suffer and feel with the little heroes and get an idea of what friends are for. The stories appeal to us and impress us emotionally. Written in a language suitable for children they offer educationally valuable pre-reading activities from discussing the different situations of the matter, which are mentioned in the books, to drawing and even acting them and so to improve the creative and linguistic abilities of our children."

"Victory isn't defined by wins or losses. It is defined by effort. If you can truthfully say, 'I did the best I could, I gave everything I had,' then you're a winner."

- Wolfgang Schadler

Lollopy Goes Olympic
 Publisher: Health Colonel Publishing, 757 SE 17th Street, #267, Fort Lauderdale, FL 33316.
954-636-5351
www.healthcolonelpublishing.com

Library of Congress Control Number: 2010915417
ISBN 978-1-935759-04-1 hardcover
ISBN 978-1-935759-06-5 softcover
ISBN 978-1-935759-07-2 eBook

Book cover design by Miranda O'Shea

◊

First Edition

LOLLOPY GOES OLYMPIC

WRITTEN BY: GRIT WEINSTEIN

ILLUSTRATIONS BY : MIRANDA O'SHEA

Lollopy is a very smart little rabbit. He loves to help others. He likes to know everything. He likes to play. He always has ideas and adventures.

Carrot Recepies
The Olympics
Psychology
©

The last time he did something good was to help the little duckling, Dory. And he was so happy about it. He and Dory became good friends.

One morning Lollopy was really surprised. There was snow everywhere. There was snow on the trees and ice on the brook. It was still snowing when he walked to the little duckling's place.

"Dory, let's build a snowman together?"

"Yes, this sounds like fun. I never saw snow in my life before!" answered the little duckling.

After a while of playing in the snow, Lollopy got an idea. “We should start our own Olympic games.” “Olympics? You mean sports and exercise? Why?” Dory is very perplexed.

Because of the snow. And what a wonderful reason to stay healthy and fit. Let's do a competition to have more fun!" answered Lollopy as he chewed on his carrot.

Well this is an excellent idea. But we need to find more competitors," suggested Dory.
"You are right. We should go and ask Sniffy, the little piglet. Maybe Oscar the turtle could be our judge," thought the little rabbit.

On their way to the farm where Sniffy lives, they met someone very interesting.

“Who are you?” asked Dory and Lollopy.

"I am Maddy. I am Paddy.We are little sheep and we do everything together," answered both at the same time.

"Where do you come from? You must be new here. Right?" asked Lollopy who always wants to know everything.

"Yes, and we live behind that hill," pointed Paddy.

"And who are you?" asked Paddy.
"My name is Dory and this is my best friend, Lollopy," introduced the little duckling.
"Hello Dory. Hello Lollopy. Nice to meet you. It's always good to have a friend," figured Maddy.

“Where are you going?” asked Paddy.
“What are you doing?” asked Maddy.
“We are on our way to visit our friend Sniffy, the little piglet. We would like to ask him if he wants to join our Olympic games!” answered Lollopy.

"Oh, this sounds like fun. Can we also join? We do everything together!" said Paddy.
"Of course you can. That would be wonderful," answered Lollopy.
All four of them continued their walk to the farm.

After they asked Sniffy and Oscar to join, the five new friends got very busy. Everybody was exercising and trying to get in shape.

Jumping jacks for Lollopy.

Ice skating practice for Dory.

Snowball rolling for Maddy and Paddy.
Hula hoop exercising for Sniffy.

Now the time finally arrived and everyone was ready. They met under a big tree, right on the frozen lake. The snow covered the meadow. And all the other animals who lived in the forest or close by, came to watch the games.

Oscar the turtle was so excited and nervous when he made his announcement. "Dear visitors! Welcome to our first animal winter Olympiad. The sports events are 100 yard downhill sliding, one loop of ice skating around the lake, 500 yard cross country skiing, snowball distance throwing and 50 yard snow shoe running.

Please welcome the competitors: Lollopy the little rabbit, Sniffy the little piglet, Maddy and Paddy the little sheep and Dory the little duckling."

Welcome
to our first animal Winter Olympiad

During the game,everybody gave his or her best, but the winner was Lollopy.
Sniffy came in last. He was very, very sad about it, because he tried so hard.
"I am a loser," said Sniffy to his friends.
"No ,you are not. And do you know why? You did it. Coming in last does not make you a loser. Yes, you lost and others won the games. But that does not make you a loser. The important thing is that you did your best and enjoyed the games with Lollopy, Maddy, Paddy and Dory. You made it through the whole game and that is something to be proud of," mentioned Lollopy who was also proud of his results.

FINISH LINE

“We are all winners, because we did the best we could and had fun together,” said Maddy.

“Yes, we are all winners and we were nice to each other, too,” said Paddy happily.

“Because I'm so proud of you, Sniffy, and because you are my friend, I will share my winning prize with you,” offered Lollopy to his friend.

FINISH LINE
1

©

"We are all winners!" rejoiced Sniffy happily.
"I did my best and I feel good about it. And I had fun with my friends."
Sniffy, Dory, Lollopy, Maddy and Paddy hugged each other and then started planning their next adventure together.

FINISH LINE

Little Cookie- House

This is an easy, quick and fun recipe. Make as many houses as you like. Use your imagination for the decoration. They are also nice as little giveaways. Your friends will love it. This is a great family project.

What you need to build five small cookie houses:

- 15 larger square graham cracker or butter cookies or ginger bread.
- Approx. 600g powdered sugar and 5 tablespoons of water or limejuice. You can use ready made icing instead, if you choose. This is the so-called “cookie glue.”
- Colorful sprinkles, marshmallows, smarties or similar.

Steps:

1) Put 5 cookies, which you will use as the bottom on one baking sheet and the other 10 cookies, which you will use as the roof, on the other.
2) Mix the powdered sugar with water or lime juice, make sure it is not too liquid, because you will use this mixture as “cookie-glue.” If it is too liquid, add more powdered sugar.
3) Cover the top of all 10 cookies with powdered sugar mix one by one, and decorate, as you like with sprinkles, marshmallows or smarties.
4) Then cover the bottom cookies thick with the powdered sugar mixture, one by one.
5) From the 10 roof cookies, take two cookies for the roof. Spread icing or powdered sugar mixture, whichever you use, on the bottom cookie so that the roof cookies will stick. Also, where the two roof cookies are touching each other on top, spread some “cookie glue” so that they will stay attached.

More Ideas:

- For more stability, “glue” a small chocolate figure or other little cookie in the middle of the bottom cookie before you put the two roof cookies on.
- Depending on what kind of cookies or crackers you are using, after few days they can become hard or very soft, but who says you always have to eat the cookie house! Another great idea is to use the cookie as table decoration. Enjoy!

Lollopy's Health & Fitness Tips

Do lots of jumping jacks

Eat lots of carrots

Bye Bye!
See you soon!

LollopyAndFriends.com

Dedications and Acknowledgements

This book is for all my friends and family, for big and little, who supported me and encouraged me to keep going. Special thanks to my husband, Bob - without his help, impossible. My mom, Irene - awesome website. To all "my" kids, your feedback has been priceless. And to my friend, Miranda, your pictures make the book rock.
Thank you.

Love Grit

I dedicate this book to Gidon, my boyfriend, who has always believed in me and supported my artistic career. To my sister, Brigid, and my mom, Helen, who always stood by my artistic creativity and have offered their continuous encouragement. To my father, John, who helped with the purchase of a new computer when my old one died. Without his help it would have been very difficult to create this book. "Grazie Papa." To my friend, Manuela, who has candidly voiced her helpful opinion. And last but not least my cat, Moon, who has always been there through my successes and my challenges.

Miranda

About the Author and Illustrator

Grit Weinstein was born and raised in Germany. After finishing her education as a nurse, she moved to Zurich, Switzerland where she lived and worked for more then 12 years. During this time, she finished her further education as Clinical Research Nurse and worked in that field to gain lots of experience. She has a passion for reading, art and children. And so, one thing leads to another. She started to write children's books. Grit lives with her husband, Lt. Col. Bob Weinstein, a well known fitness instructor and author in South Florida, where she not only enjoys the sunny weather, she is also working on new children books, her art skills and on her Florida State Nursing License. For more Information go to www.GritWeinstein.com and www.LollopyAndFriends.com

Miranda O'Shea was raised in Rome, Italy for most of her early years. She has had a mixed education with a combination of Italian and English. From Rome, Miranda went on to further her studies in England, and studied fashion design. She then went on to Santa Barbara, California to study fine art and multimedia. She has had her own greeting card business photographing architectural views around parts of the globe. She resides in South Florida with her boyfriend, Gidon, and has a line of baby t-shirts with her colorful illustrations. For more information go to www.MirandaOshea.info and www.LollopyAndFriends.com

Already Available!

Coming Soon!

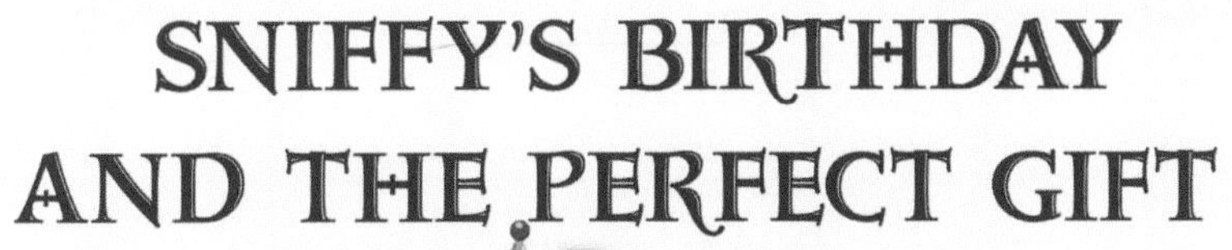
SNIFFY'S BIRTHDAY
AND THE PERFECT GIFT

WRITTEN BY: GRIT WEINSTEIN
ILLUSTRATIONS BY : MIRANDA O'SHEA

"There's nothing that can help you understand your beliefs more than trying to explain them to an inquisitive child. ~ Frank A. Clark

Lollopy and Friends Products

www.LollopyandFriends.com

The Tale of the Little Duckling
Color illustrations story book for 4 to 8 year olds
Softcover, $14.95, ISBN 978-0-9841783-8-4
Hardcover, $16.95, ISBN 978-1-935759-00-3
eBook, $5.99, ISBN 978-0-984-17839-1 (all formats)

Lollopy Goes Olympic
Color illustrations story book for 4 to 8 year olds
Softcover, $14.95, ISBN 978-1-935759-06-5
Hardcover, $16.95, ISBN 978-1-935759-04-1
eBook, $5.99, ISBN 978-1-935759-07-2 (all formats)

Tote Bags, Mugs, Buttons, Mousepads and more
Lollopy and Friends
www.LollopyandFriends.com

Personalized T-Shirts by Miranda O'Shea
Children's Book Illustrator
www.MirandaOShea.info

HEALTHCOLONELPUBLISHING.COM

Helping our children learn important life lessons.

QUICK ORDER FORM

Fax orders: 866-481-2804. Send this form.

Telephone orders: Call 888-768-9892 toll-free

Email orders: thehealthcolonel@beachbootcamp.net

Postal orders: The Health Colonel, Lt. Col. Bob Weinstein, USAR-Ret., 757 SE 17th Street, #267, Fort Lauderdale, FL 33316, Telephone 954-636-5351

Please send the following books, audio CDs, DVDs:

Please send more FREE information on:

- ❑ Other books
- ❑ Speaking/seminars
- ❑ Fitness Boot Camp
- ❑ Mailing Lists

Name:

Address:

City: State: Zip:

Telephone:

Email address:

Sales tax: Please add Florida sales tax for products shipped to Florida addresses.

Shipping:
U.S.: $4.50 for first book, CD or DVD and $2.50 for each additional product.
International: $9.50 for first product; $5.50 for each additional product (estimate).

LaVergne, TN USA
24 March 2011
221301LV00002B

* 9 7 8 1 9 3 5 7 5 9 0 6 5 *